GM FOODS

Kate McArthur

GM Foods

Text: Kate McArthur
Editor: Rebecca Crisp
Design: Jess Kelly
Series design: James Lowe
Photo researcher: Corrina Tauschke
Production controller: Adam Bextream
Reprint: Siew Han Ong

Acknowledgements
The author and publisher would like to acknowledge permission to reproduce material from the following sources:
Alamy/Lisa Barber: p. 17; Corbis/David Turnley: p. 20; Corbis/Peter Dench: pp. 6–7; Fotolia/Arrow Studio: p. 14; Getty Images: pp. 1, 15, cover, back cover; iStockphoto/Arthur Kwiatkowski: p. 11 (top); iStockphoto/Klaudia Steiner: p. 11 (bottom); iStockphoto/Lev Ezhov: p. 12 (main); iStockphoto/Stacey Newman: p. 12 (inset); Photolibrary: p. 10; Photolibrary/Diaphor La Phototheque: p. 5; Photolibrary/Garry D McMichael: p. 13 (top);Photolibrary/Javier Larrea: pp. 4, 13 (bottom right); Photolibrary/LLA: pp. 3, 21; Photolibrary/Lynn Stone: p. 6 (right); Photolibrary/Mark Sykes/SPL: p. 19; Photolibrary/Photo Researchers: p. 18 (top right); Photolibrary/Picture Partners: p. 16; Photolibrary/Randy Faris: pp. 22–23; Photolibrary/Richard Hutchings: p. 18 (top left); Photolibrary/Ripp: p. 18 (bottom); Photolibrary/Robin Smith: p. 6 (left), Richard Morden © Cengage Learning Australia: pp. 8–9 .

Fast Forward Independent Texts
Level 21

For product information and technology assistance,
in Australia call 1300 790 853;
in New Zealand call 0508 635 766

For permission to use material from this text or product,
please email **aust.permissions@cengage.com**

ISBN 978 0 17 018004 7
ISBN 978 0 17 017899 0 (set)

Cengage Learning Australia
Level 7, 80 Dorcas Street
South Melbourne, Victoria Australia 3205

Cengage Learning New Zealand
Unit 4B Rosedale Office Park
331 Rosedale Road, Albany, North Shore NZ 0632

For learning solutions, visit **cengage.com.au**

Printed in Australia by Ligare Pty Ltd
3 4 5 6 7 25 24 23 22

Contents

CHAPTER 1

Food for Thought

Over the last 15 years,
there has been a lot of discussion
about whether or not genetically modified (GM) foods
are good for people and the planet.

Foods that are genetically modified have been changed from the way that they would normally grow in nature.

GM foods are not created or grown naturally, like other foods.

Genetically modified foods are not as new as most people might think.

For thousands of years, farmers have been improving the features of many different plants and animals by **breeding** them with other, better plants and animals.

Many modern apple trees have been genetically modified so that they do not grow very tall.

This process is known as selective breeding and can take thousands of years to cause big changes in plants or animals.

a beef cow

Over the years, some cows have been bred for eating and some for milking.

a milk cow

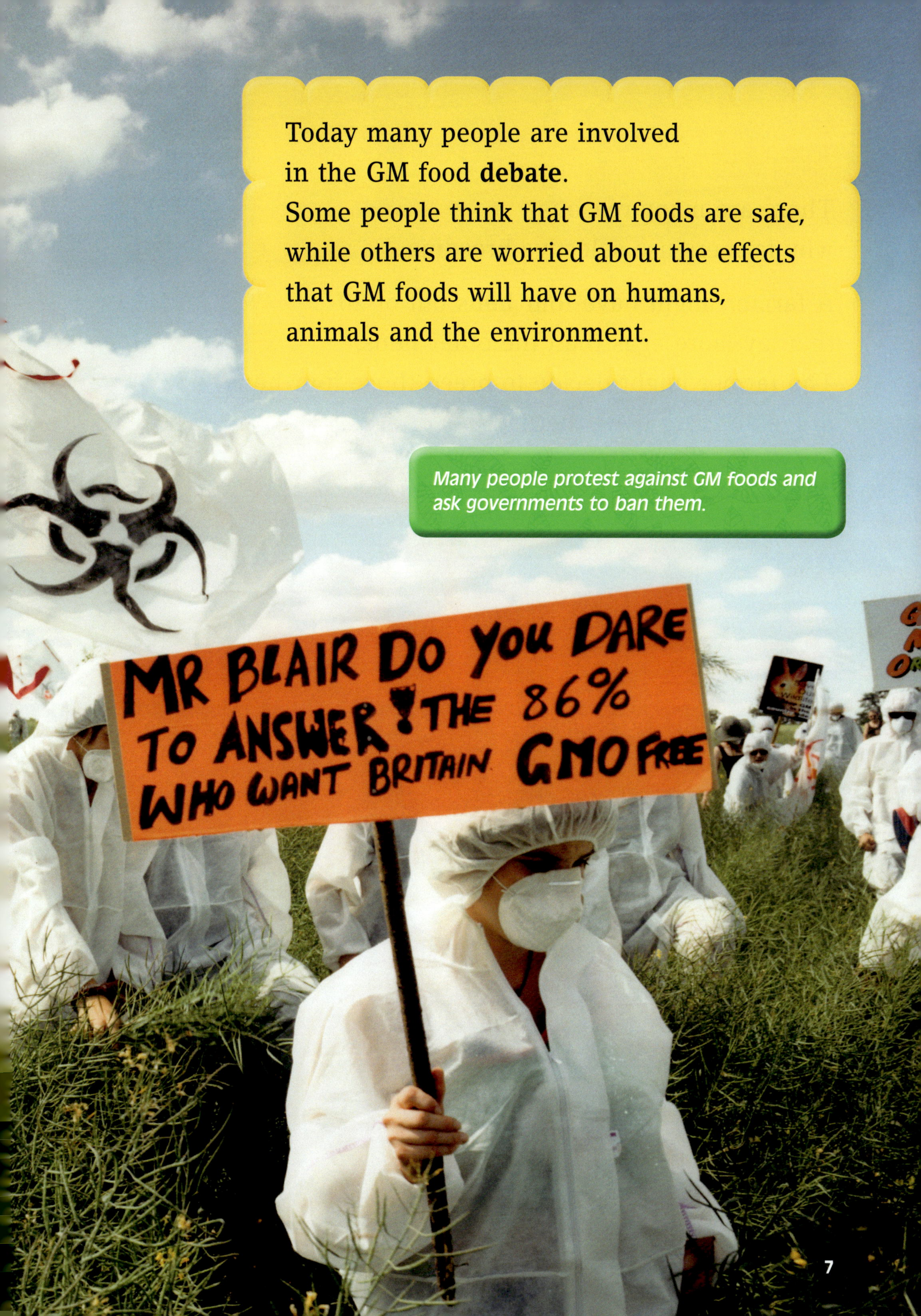

Today many people are involved in the GM food **debate**.
Some people think that GM foods are safe, while others are worried about the effects that GM foods will have on humans, animals and the environment.

Many people protest against GM foods and ask governments to ban them.

CHAPTER 2

Creating GM Foods

There are many reasons why farmers use selective breeding.

A farmer might have four **hens** out of 20 that lay more eggs than the other hens. The farmer might decide to breed those four hens to create more hens that lay lots of eggs.

Selective breeding of chickens has produced hens that lay lots of eggs.

The farmer selects the hens that lay the most eggs.

This process would already have been used by **generations** of farmers to create hens that produced lots of eggs.

But scientists in a laboratory can make these kinds of changes much faster.

The best breeding hen and a rooster produce hens that lay even more eggs.

Even though selective breeding is not what we think of today when we hear the term “genetically modified”, the goals and the results are similar.

However, there are still many differences between the two processes.

The main difference today is that **genes** from species that are not even related can now be put together. For example, a gene from a red fish can be added to a tomato plant to make future tomatoes look redder. This is not possible with selective breeding.

CHAPTER 3

The Benefits of GM Foods

There are many reasons why some people think that GM foods are a good idea.

First, some GM crops, such as potatoes and corn, have been developed so that they can grow without much water. This means that these crops can be grown in countries that do not get much rain.

GM crops like potatoes and corn can grow well in dry countries or during a drought.

Second, some GM foods do not need to be sprayed with **insecticides**.
This means that farmers do not need to spend money to buy these chemicals.
It is also better for the environment and for people who eat these foods.

Some GM foods are resistant to pests, so they do not need to be sprayed with chemicals.

Third, scientists say that GM foods could contain **vaccines** in the future. This would mean that children could be vaccinated against diseases just by eating an apple.

If food contained vaccines, people may not have to have immunisation injections.

GM food companies are required
to test their products.
But, people who support GM foods
say that there is no proof
that genetically modified crops cause damage
to humans or the planet.

CHAPTER 4

The Risks of GM Foods

There are many reasons why other people think that GM foods are a bad idea.

First, these people say that GM foods could be very dangerous for humans and animals. Some animals have developed serious health problems after eating GM corn and grain.

If a cow gets sick after eating GM food, its meat might not be safe for humans to eat.

Second, the companies that own the technology to create GM crops could take over the food market and raise prices. If only GM crops are grown in the future, these companies could charge farmers huge amounts of money to buy the seeds for these crops.

Third, mixing genes from animals and plants causes problems for religious people and people with special diets. For example, if a pig gene is added to an apple, some Jewish people could not eat that apple, because they are not supposed to eat pork.

Some Jewish people do not eat pork.

Some Hindu people do not eat beef.

Vegetarians do not eat meat, and vegans do not eat any animal products at all.

Finally, people who are against GM foods argue that scientists cannot know all the problems that might develop if people start growing and eating only GM foods. And science might be moving too quickly to stop the damage that could be done.

CHAPTER 5

Weighing Up the Arguments

People who support GM foods say that genetic modification will solve the problem of world hunger by protecting plants and animals.

These people do not have enough food to eat because their crops died.

But people who are against GM foods fear that they will damage people's health and destroy the environment.

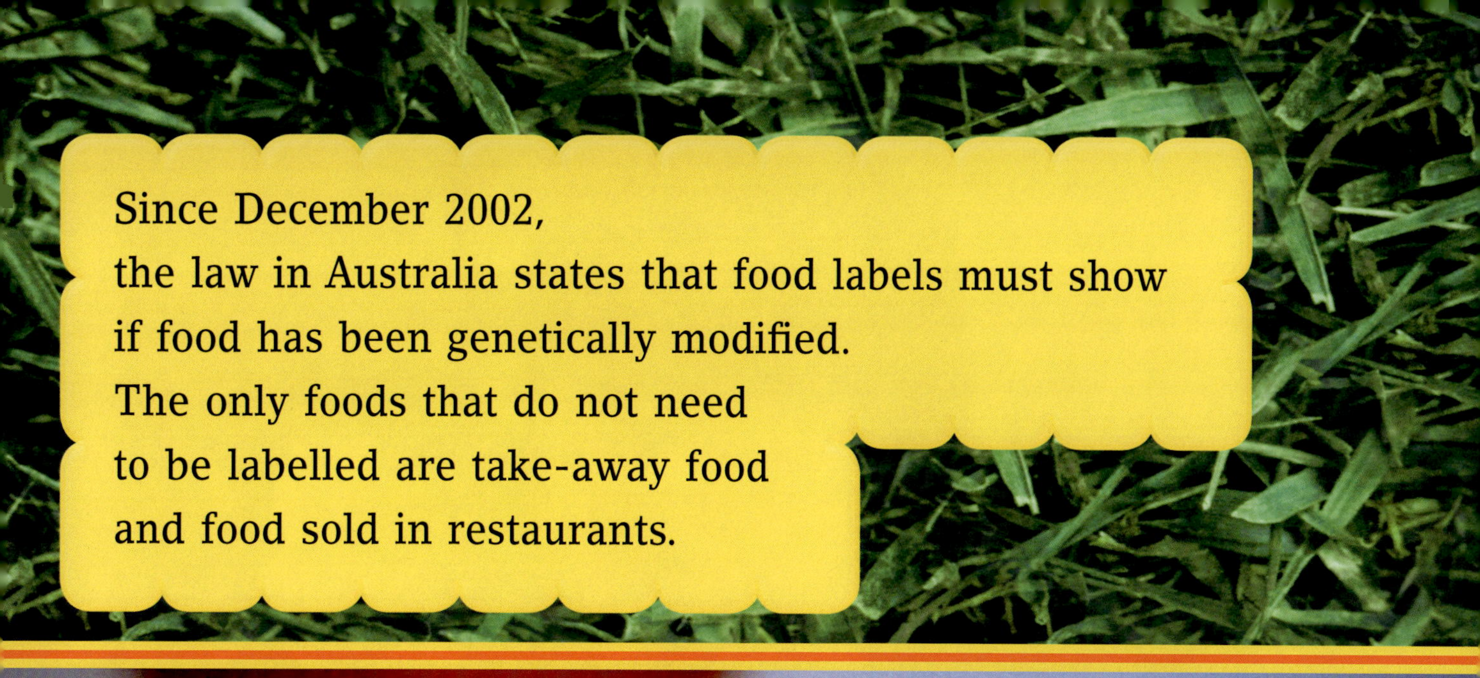

Since December 2002,
the law in Australia states that food labels must show if food has been genetically modified.
The only foods that do not need to be labelled are take-away food and food sold in restaurants.

There is still a lot of **research** to do before scientists can know if GM foods are good or bad for humans and the environment.
It may take years to find out about any dangers.

Until then, foods in Australia will carry a label if they contain genetically modified ingredients. That way, people have enough facts to decide if they are happy to eat these foods or not.

Glossary

breeding bringing two animals together to reproduce

debate a discussion of two or more points of view

generations groups of people born around the same time

genes tiny carriers of information that are passed on from one generation to the next, and that control features like eye colour and height

hens female chickens

insecticides chemicals that are sprayed on plants to kill the insects that eat them

research careful study or investigation

vaccines medicines that give increased protection from a particular disease

Index